Beyond the Graveyard
Ghostly Encounters

Narrative Poetry

by

L. Buckley

NIGHT EDGE PUBLISHING

*"When One Coffin Closes,
Another One Opens."*

Spirits roam far beyond the graveyard in this
haunting collection of verse told ghost tales.

Night Edge Publishing

Copyright © 2020 L. Buckley

Edited by Jenuine Blu

Cover Design by Cotseres Images:
www.cotseresimages.com

ISBN-13: 978-1-7352356-1-5

Printed in the Unites States of America

Dedicated to my late Grandma, Julia.
A nurturing woman.
A kind person.
A creative force.
A heart-centered poet whose lyrical end rhymes
delivered meaningful messages.
&
To those who bravely explore the unknown.

Content

Acknowledgments

Heartfelt thanks to my husband Tom for his support, encouragement, and willingness to read manuscripts in their infancy. His insights always bring forth clarity. Warmest thanks to my cousin Michael for graciously listening to poetry for the last six months, and for believing in this little book of ghost stories. And to my beautiful friend and fellow author, Miracle Austin, thank you for your ears, guidance, and excitement. Your positive energy helped light the path onward.

Introduction

I've always had interest in ghosts. In what they represent symbolically, such as haunting memories, and dreams and goals that evade or ghost us, and in contemplating if they exist. Based on my experiences, I believe they do. Not the exaggerated versions depicted in movies and books, but much subtler. However, I've lived in a haunted house complete with electronic disruptions, moving objects, foul odors, and apparitions we'd catch in our periphery. After months of desperate conversations with the ghosts or whatever caused the chaos about how we had to share space, they eventually stopped acting out.

Early, 2019, I started feeling ill. Fatigue, along with a lot of other random symptoms. By July, 2019, my symptoms worsened. None of my doctor's appointments revealed answers, which added to my building stress. One anxious night, I smelled my grandmother. A scent uniquely hers, followed by a flood of loving remembrances. Her aroma, the sense she was close, and the fond memories brought me comfort.

Her visits during difficult times has gone on since she passed away over three decades ago.

Wish I could think her here, but that doesn't seem to be how it works. If it is her, she presents herself on her terms, not mine, yet her timing is always spot on.

My grandmother used to write short poems. She'd dealt with her own health issues and found writing thoughtful, uncomplicated poetry relaxing. She inspired this book. As did her terms, visiting when she wants, not when I ask.

With her in mind, I jotted down narrative, verse poems, and similarly experienced calmness. Rather than search and plot and struggle, I followed my grandmother's lead. Sat quietly at the desk and let the stories come to me. A simple word or vague image would strike me, and I'd run with it. Many of the stories felt as if they wrote themselves. They flowed, and I transcribed. An experiment in crafting whatever popped in my head without any idea how they'd end.

By November, 2019, I was diagnosed with Stage 3 Cancer. Having the poems to focus on kept me sane. As I write this Intro, I'm on chemotherapy. Soon, I'll be a cancer survivor. After surgery and completing my chemo treatments, my outcome looks great. I'll still require tests yearly for some time, but after this scary ordeal, the checkups will be a cinch.

Speaking of scary, I often get asked why I'm into horror and dark fiction. It's been a lifelong draw. As a kid, I'd skip playing outside with friends to watch black and white Vincent Price horror shows. There were several scary weekend specials, but I liked Vincent Price so much, I had expected to name my first son Vincent. Didn't manifest, only because I never had a son.

For the most part, I think we horror buffs are wired slightly different. We appreciate the adrenaline rush of scares, twists, and surprises. Slower paced horror offers an adrenaline rush too, cleverly stretching out the suspense, and somber horror tugs our heartstrings, doing so with the edginess we crave. And when the movie is over, or we close the book, having been affected, we're left with much to talk about, and tougher skin. It's my opinion, darker tales often help us deal with darker realities.

Whether you're drawn to eerie ghost stories, or poems, I hope this collection provides plenty of chills and entertainment.

Advice

Here's a lesson when it comes to the dead,
valuable information to store in your head.
So if you encounter a ghost you won't dread,
but, instead, act based on what I've said.
Spirits are kind of like fish in the sea,
all very different, unique as can be.
Some wander forever, aimlessly,
while others feel content and free.
And many think they're trapped, endlessly,
searching for a key,
to flee,
and go where? Don't ask me.
Some ghosts are vicious and intend to scare.
Don't know why, wish they'd make me aware.
Do they have to be such a nightmare?
Floating through the air, an invisible grizzly bear,
growling and throwing objects, tempers flare.
Leave them alone, go away, beware.
They're obviously troubled,
and in death, their anger doubled.
Existing in the Otherworld, contained or bubbled,
they're cranky and spooky, always ruffled.

Those are the ghosts you want to avoid.

They're already annoyed, under-joyed, and paranoid.

And then there's the misplaced who don't realize they've moved on,

gliding between worlds with the grace of a swan.

One minute they had clarity, the next they came upon,

changes they sensed, but couldn't fully grasp the obscure phenomenon.

They're puzzled, but usually not considered a threat.

Disoriented, maybe clumsy, because they just don't get

anything is peculiar, yet, it is... so they're upset.

Harmless, though, if you should meet one, don't fret.

Which leads me to those consciously roaming another plain,

they've come to terms, surrendered their emotional strain,

imitating kings and queens, mysterious turf they reign.

Living in a dreamlike state, their new normal, their domain.

Those types of ghosts communicate in various
ways,
kind and inquisitive, or devious shadow plays.
They're individuals, their personality is what
sways
them to be social, or behave like rebellious
castaways.
But if you come across one who's comfortable
with endlessness,
confident but not displaying aggressiveness,
how you respond will be your guess.
Keep calm, don't stress, as you progress.
Education in ghosts is an ongoing process.
Sometimes we don't know what we'll do until
we're tested.
Pay attention to the cues I previously suggested.
Probably could have explained faster, less time
invested.
I'm a chatty ghost, a talker, unrested.
Bottom line, not overdone...
Scary ghosts, you should run.
Bewildered ghosts, dull as a stale bun.
Self-assured ghosts, stick around, could be fun.
And if by chance you're trying to reach a departed
loved one,
I offer a secret as grand as the sun.

You don't need a gravesite or special location, just love, eagerness, and concentration.

Diary

June, Saturday, (anniversary of my accident),
I was texting, never mind, don't want to relive the
event.
Today I went with my friends to the mall,
got towels for the beach, swimsuits and a
volleyball.
Stopped for ice cream, everyone ordered chocolate
but me.
My favorites are vanilla, pistachio, and cherry.
Took some selfies in front of a mannequin
dressed like a mermaid with a shell top and a
sparkly fin.
Sat in a parking lot and talked for a while,
mostly about a kid in school too insecure to smile.
Some of my friends shot a video for TikTok,
mimicking seagulls circling the dock.
Dusk arrived and our group parted ways,
except for two of us, my friend came with me to
spend a few days.

Snuck in my room to write that page,
but I know what will happen, based on history, I
can gauge.

My friend will snoop in my private book, scream and cry,

show some older woman my accounts and ask why...

...And ask how, and where,

and is it possible for her every action to just appear,

in a diary she said was hidden in the wall.

But she's the nosy one, to get to it she had to crawl.

She reads it every night, sitting solo,

claims there's a spirit in her bedroom trailing her, although,

not sure what type of ghost would hang out with us.

We don't do anything exciting, plus,

someone would feel a presence or find weird things,

ghosts aren't angels, they don't have wings.

They'd cling to the ethers, make noises, leave clues they were here.

Relocate belongings, make little items like jewelry disappear.

My friend finally fell asleep; I'm returning my diary to the wall.

And then I'll borrow her silver locket, she won't notice, it's small.

Siblings

"Do you remember when I died?"

"I'll never forget. Wept for a year. The longest I've cried."

"What about when I was born?"

"You were first. They said you had the vocals of a wailing horn."

"What about your big mouth, what did they say?"

"I came delicate as a ballerina in a ballet."

"Haha, sure. Your voice can fill a football arena."

"Funny coming from someone who laughs like a hyena."

"Whatever. My style was cool."

"They still talk about it in school."

"Tell me again how I died."

"Let's not go there. I was horrified."

"Death isn't pretty, you know that."

"Neither is acne, but it doesn't claw my soul like a deranged rat."

"I died too young, would you agree?"

"Of course, why the pain is so beastly."

"What did you do on the day of my death?"

"I went into shock, couldn't catch my breath."

"And now, how do you spend your time without me?"

"I sit, waiting for you in unbearable misery."

"They say you've shut down, but that isn't true."

"No, it's not, unlike me, they can't see you."

"Not even death could tear us apart."

"That's right. We're eternally joined at the heart."

Observer

You can't see me, this I know.
As it should be, my circumstances aren't for
show.
But I watch you, same way you might study your
peers
at school, or neighbors, with open eyes and ears.
We embolden each other, good and bad.
I've been watching for a century and honestly I'm
glad,
I'm not in your era, here and now,
seems overwhelming, I don't know how,
you conduct your daily, busy routine,
with information flooding your phone screen.
I'm aware of the device you grip with all your
might,
on it most of the day, and throughout the night.
You've probably gathered I'm not among the
living.
No worries, I happen to be extremely forgiving.
My heart stopped on my sixteenth year,
I died a decent person, my conscience was clear.
Agreeably, my landscape is vague and curious.

If you knew what I thought of your realm, you'd
be furious.
Cruelty, meanness, or what's termed, trolling,
on those electronic devices, no one's patrolling.
When I come across someone unsavory,
callous people who lack even a sliver of bravery.
The ones on their keyboard pushing lies and hate,
hiding behind Anonymous, difficult to locate.
Not for me, my range is vast.
I can affect a person fairly fast.
First a chill, small hairs stand erect,
muscles ache, a presence they detect.
As I kite closer I see the vein in their neck,
pulsing up and down as they check
their surroundings for what makes them uneasy.
Never fathoming I'm why they're queasy.
I crush without touching, shrinking their space,
something they feel but cannot trace.
When I exhale, my breath scrapes their skin.
They nervously wipe their legs, arms, and chin.
Then bounce in place, a scared kangaroo,
panting and nauseas, they perceive it's not the flu.
They look to the ceiling, sides, and floor,
frantically search their house door to door.
I follow, emitting an odor they can't deny,

one I captured during decay, it's putrid, they often cry.

Coughing and gagging they're hunched over and ill,

but the true sickness comes from their poisonous pill.

They project onto others belittlement and fear,

so when I terrify them into a corner by simply being there,

they whine and beg me to stop, attempt to lie low,

but I've been watching them, they're the ones who need to go.

As I've mentioned earlier, I'm a forgiving ghost.

My mark though, is indelible, causing madness for most.

Bully

A few years ago, on my route to and from school,
I crossed a bridge over a lake bluer than our pool.
My friends used to say the bridge was home to a
ghost,
who'd stand near the railing like a sheer
lamppost.
I never saw any such thing,
just plain old cement same color as my
shoestring.
Here's the crazy part, and you should probably
sit,
because it finally happened, but I've kept it secret.
There was a kid in my English class who picked
on the rest of us.
In the halls and outside, he'd push, spit, and cuss.
A deranged boy, he never demonstrated guilt or
regret
when he injured a classmate, teacher, or pet.
He knocked me down a couple of times, but I
ignored him,
got up, refused to be a victim.
He didn't like that I wasn't afraid.
I shuddered, but chose not to be played.

Never revealed my fears, tears, or cares,
or scabs from him flicking my ears.
Which he hated and it only made things worse.
Didn't tell my parents, or he'd put me in a hearse.
Keeping my mouth shut—big mistake.
Every bone in my body he threatened to break.
He wasn't lying, he set his sights on me.
After school, he followed, barking, "You'll end up
food for a ducky!"
And he'd say "Ducky" with the force of a dizzying
hit.
The power of words we shouldn't omit.
The thought of starving beaks picking me apart,
terrified me, the kid had no heart.
I got to the bridge, the tool huffing down my
neck,
his anger seared, my nerves were a wreck.
We headed up the bridge, me not knowing what
to do,
his unreasonable rage proved he lacked a screw or
two.
Like a dream, near the safety rail, the rumored
ghost did appear,
in a baseball cap my friend from eighth grade
used to wear.

A sports fanatic and admired student, he vanished like stolen bling,
no one could find him; thrusted our town into mourning.
But there he was, I yelled out his name.
And then the future criminal punched me with perfect aim.
I folded over struggling for air.
He said, "It's going to get awful for you, I promise, I swear."
He body slammed me, wrapped his hands around my throat.
I couldn't breathe, no kidding, no joke.
He said, "I don't know why you shouted that name,
you'll be sorry, you won't win this game."
My head pounded, my vision grew blurry,
through the haze, the ghost approached in a hurry.
Suddenly the death grip around my neck ended.
I assumed the juvenile delinquent had been apprehended.
Applied pressure to my arm to slow blood from a gash.
Wheezed after hearing a disturbingly loud splash.
I stumbled to my feet trembling and upset.

The ghost stared at the horizon, a hat on a transparent silhouette.

Currently, I'm on the bridge gazing at the water.

The memory came back thanks to a splashing otter...

And a flock of wildfowl a grade school terrorizer swore would eat me,

like they did my friend who expected an apology, which never came, so down to the duckies went our bully.

Finder

Middle of the night, a pebble taps my bedroom
window.
I'm wide awake, just came in from the patio.
Rough day at work, a good friend got fired,
which kept me up, tossing and wired.
The few hours I slept were infested with
nightmares.
And now someone's outside, downstairs.
Peek through the glass, look below.
Unbelievable, it's a special person I know.
She ran away last year, allegedly.
Devastating for everyone, draining, emotionally.
My heartbeat quickens, excited to see,
she's okay, alive, and smiley.
Throw on some clothes, dart outside.
Fog hides the mountains, she stands doe-eyed.
I say, "You're home, back in town.
Your folks are worried sick. Do they know you're
around?"
"Yeah," she nods, "I've already checked in.
Couldn't wait to see you. Share where I've been."
Didn't want to depress the mood,

but she broke my heart, spent six months in solitude.

"What makes you think you can come back to me,

without an explanation, your eyes all sad and twinkly?"

Fog twists around her frame,

nothing between us will ever be the same.

Encapsulated by night, I want to hold her, tell her she's safe.

My anger dissolves, she's fragile, a waif.

"I'm interested in where you've been. I want you to show me.

It's dark out here, tomorrow we'll sightsee.

Tonight, let's rest, you can have my bed.

We'll finish this in the morning, big day ahead."

"No," she says, "I won't be satisfied,

until you know why I left, then you can decide,

whether to dump me or forgive me, simple as that.

Grab a flashlight, the terrain isn't flat."

Before I can argue, she vanishes in the fog.

I snatch the flashlight from behind a fake frog.

Click it on, slice through the dense mist,

aim it on her backside, the watch I gave her still on her wrist.

She says, "You'll understand when we get there.
I'm taking you someplace incredible, nothing like
it anywhere.
Personally, I think it has magical powers.
Time passes fast, minutes unknowingly become
hours."
We carefully tread further, my flashlight
zigzagging in front.
I recognize our surroundings, remembering my
last hunt.
Boulders and forest, strands of ivy hug trees.
The air smells muddy, stagnant, no wind or
breeze.
I know the area like the back of my hand,
yet I'm feeling uncertain about this patch of land.
Seems we're entering uncharted territory,
beyond the old mines and ancient quarry.
We shuffle through dewy leaves and dirt.
I'm vigilant, don't want her to get hurt.
She stops, stares forward in a daze.
We've completed our tiring walk through the
maze.
"This is it," she says with a huff.
Then adds, "You've been kept in the dark long
enough."

Literally, I think, shining my light on the mystery place,
which turns out to be a cavern, yawning mouth at its base.
Before I could speak, she speeds to the cave.
My pulse increases, she lures me in with a wave.
I follow her through a long dark tunnel,
starts spacious but begins to funnel.
Spits us out into a nice sized space.
Dingy and frigid, but I keep a straight face.
"Isn't it amazing? The embedded jewels sparkle bright.
The frothy pond from the waterfall—I could listen to it all night.
Dazzling moths glowing like lavender stars.
This is why I stayed. *My* hideaway is now ours."
Nothing she said makes sense, in fact, none of it is true.
I scan the gritty walls with the flashlight to view.
No sparkly treasures, or pond, or wild-winged insects.
How was she seeing these nonexistent objects?
"We should go," I say thinking the worst.
Maybe she's on drugs, or fell from a ledge, headfirst.
She needs a doctor, medical care.

"We'll come back in daylight, when everything's clear."

I wiggle my flashlight, didn't see her at all.

Won't let her go again, "Come on," I desperately call.

The silence is unsettling; I trace her soiled footprints.

She's attempting to pull another one of her disappearing stints.

"I'm over here," she bellows from the other end of a passageway.

"What's it going to be? Dump me, or forgive me and stay?"

Feeling claustrophobic, acids curdle in my gut.

Pacing cautiously, got myself into this rut.

Forgot how much she means to me until I saw her smile.

If this is where she wants to be, we can camp here for a while.

Reach a clump of something I can't immediately discern.

I step closer and my reality takes a hellish turn.

My breath seizes,

every muscle freezes.

I see the watch I gave her, exhale ghastly moans.

It's attached to her decomposing body, she's practically all bones.

Mirror

Me and my girls meet in the alley,
to talk about school and the upcoming pep rally.
There's a basement nearby but we don't dare look
in the windows.
The building's haunted, a fact everyone knows.

Me and my girls gather here in the basement,
to support each other through our supernatural
displacement.
There's a couple of windows but we won't peek
through the glass.
People in the alley are scary, no class.

The sun shines bright, we all hover in the shade.
I'm thinking about the ghosts while my best
spotter fixes her braid.
Supposedly, the building used to be a furniture
store,
and the employee's kids were there for a tour.
They were murdered we're told, butchered like
cattle,
which is why they seek revenge, why they want to
battle.

Our new forever home used to be a private health club.
Me and my friends snuck in after closing, no payment stub.
We were gossiping in the locker room unaware of a gas leak,
which before the fumes overtook us, made us tired, fuzzy, and weak.
We're fine where we are because alley people pick fights.
Stomping and hollering, weekdays and nights.

We practice a few chants, poses, and cheers,
shape our arms into vees and spheres.
Next week the competing team will come to challenge us,
might as well be clowns in that lemon-yellow school bus.
This time they think they're going to win.
Can't be done, we're tough, they're skin is thin.
"We are the champions," we scream in the alley,
"They can't beat us, those basics from the valley!"

Here in the basement from a distance we see,
the horrifying girls outside yelling viciously.
I'm curious though, why they're so mean and loud,
why isn't their screeching drawing a crowd?

They're bullies, I'm sure, that's why they're roaring.
Doing whatever they can to avoid being boring.
Showing off, trying to scare whoever's ignoring
them and their threats and their hunger for
warring.

As our meeting concludes I'm wondering why,
the ghosts in the basement are so quiet and sly.
Those are the types that can't be trusted or
forgotten,
they like sneak attacks, anything shifty and
rotten.
Think I'll find strength and peek in the window.
Show them they can't intimidate us, we won't go.
A bunch of us step toward the dirty glass,
we're freaking out; we're not walking fast.

We'll be here forever, in this cool, murky place,
it's secure here, unlike out there with the human
race.
Once long ago we were made of flesh and bones.
Now we're vaporous, misty unknowns.
One annoyance we shouldn't allow to continue,
are the screamers in the alley, there must be
something we can do.
We'll glide to the window, see what they're up to.
Plan our next move, a strategy to pursue.

We reach the window and stare inside.
Faces look back, my heart thumps, I'm terrified!
They're bodiless, misshaped, and sheer as a light veil,
with inset onyx eyes, and their coloring is pale.

We reach the window and stare outside.
Faces look back, my aura tingles, I'm terrified!
They're alive in skin too thick to see through,
with bulging eyes and sweaty cheeks, ew.

Me and my girls jump backwards real quick.
The ghosts would have killed us using some hereafter trick.
I knew they were wicked, they must be, they're dead.
Yeah, we're out of here, we've got brains in our head.

Me and my girls thrust backwards with the power of a sneeze.
The living would have banished us using earthly novelties.
I knew they were wicked, they must be, they're breathing.
Most of the living are frustrated and seething.

Not going back,
situations too whack.
But if we do,
we'll stay out of view.
Problem solved - We've evolved.

Not peeking out the window again,
too unsafe, period the end.
But if we do,
next time we'll shout: BOO!
Problem solved – We'll get involved.

Chosen

Casper is friendly, up for child's play.
My visiting ghost doesn't act that way.
It howls and giggles maniacally every night.
Flings my shoes, turns on and off the light.
I've hid under blankets, but then it gnawed my toes.
In debilitating terror, I took on a statue pose.
Scary crap you have to admit,
I power through, I don't quit.
Occasionally, there's blotchy fingerprints on my phone.
And once when dad wasn't home, it typed *I know you're alone.*
Not sure why it picked me to haunt,
but soon the tables will turn, I'll find it and daunt.
I've decided to become a serious ghost hunter,
kick mean spirits out of this world like a pro football punter.
It'll take some time to learn the ropes.
Believe me when I tell you, I have high hopes.
Meanwhile, I'll be cautious and smart,
squeeze lemon juice on my feet, for this toe biting ghost to taste tart.

I'll put decoys in my closet and under the bed.
Give it some challenges, a throb in its head.
We'll either forge an alliance or it'll go on its own,
or face me later when my spirit hunter skills are
sharp and tone.

Linger

Sat in the cafeteria having lunch with my friends,
talking about apps, boys, and the latest fashion
trends.
Didn't have anything to say, I was still a bit
stunned.
Had a fender bender on my way to school, felt
kind of numb.
Which started a conversation about a girl each of
us knew,
who died in a car wreck because of a red light
another driver blew.
We missed this girl who used to make everyone
laugh.
She took the best selfies, loved to photograph.
She intended to be a lawyer, handle tough cases,
travel the world, experience lots of places.
Greece, Spain, Canada too.
There was so much she had planned to do.
We all grieved her life ended too soon,
because of an oblivious speeding buffoon.
I picked up a pop bottle and everyone screamed.
They thought I would spill it, that's how it
seemed.

Then one of my friends mentioned this girl's
unusual scar,
near her elbow, shaped like a guitar.
She'd gotten it as a toddler in a park on a slide,
a battle wound, she'd fool around, feigning pride.
The room started spinning, my stomach turned.
The girl they spoke of I slowly learned,
was me, oh my god—the dead girl is me.
I'm what I wasn't expecting to be.
A recurrent story. A memory. A student for all
eternity.

Haunted

There's something about a moonless night,
that gives squeamish people a chilling fright.
Not me, it's when I feel most alive,
searching for spirits who continue to thrive.
I circulate this neglected house netted in cobwebs
and dust,
slow careful steps, the corroded floor crunching
like crust.
BOOM!
I hear from another room.
Crane my neck, then head toward the noise,
through the archway, see a bunch of shivering
girls and boys.
They're huddled together, gliding like sludge.
I catch up, give them a nudge.
"HEY!" I yell unmistakably, so they understand.
They scream bloody murder and quickly disband.
Each one racing for the front door,
out they run, they'd been here before.
This time they'll never come back,
and I can be in peace where I dwell, in the
blackest of black.

Vision

Robot.
That's what I heard.
But no one sits with me at the river save for a
bird.
It didn't come from my phone,
I know, because I intentionally left it at home,
to sit in tranquility, be alone.
Stifled by sadness, mostly feeling different than
my peers.
Came to a quiet place to hide my salty tears.
But once that word, *Robot*, droned in my ears,
it stimulated my mind and all its gears.
Decide my imagination must have sent a helpful
hint.
In my dismal state, I'd gained a glint.
The fresh scented water reflects the clouds,
my greatest ideas come when I separate from
crowds.
Dig within and I'm immediately caught,
in a bottomless spiral of thought.
At last, the brainteaser clicks like a finished
puzzle.

I squeal, then cover my mouth with my hand, an unconscious muzzle.

The message developed clear and wise,
if we're all similar, we're Robots, not an option, shedding my disguise.

Determined to figure out exactly who I am,
avoid being a Robot, copycat, or scam.

Eventually, I'd get comfortable in my own skin.
My happiness is worth fighting for, self-love is where to begin.

Suddenly, near the river's edge a few steps away,
an apparition appears, translucent and grey.

As the scene sharpens, it's absolutely a boy,
holding an object, some type of toy.

And now he looks alive, his life streaming like a movie.

He runs to the water ahead of his parents to prove he...

...wasn't too young to have independent fun?
The river ripples and underneath a mild wave,
something grabs his attention, he walks in, steadfast and brave.

He leans forward, smiles, and fishes out his find.
The toy his spirit holds today, followed by an event unkind.

Before he trips and drowns in that very spot,

he clutches the plastic plaything, snickers, and
says: *Robot*.

Medium

Not easy being me, I have no choice.
I hear the dead speak, plainly, as if they have a
voice.
Born with this gift, it started at age five.
I was contacted by a being, human, but not alive.
A being because it wasn't a person,
more, a tingly sensation that would increasingly
worsen.
My fingers and toes would tickle and buzz,
right before I'd hear someone talk, and because
I was too afraid to connect; I sheltered under my
bed.
Didn't matter, the crazy things they said.
Stuff like, "Help me," "Where am I?" and "Who
are you?"
I finally replied, "You tell me, I'm curious too."
By the time I turned twelve I had it under control.
Hired by grievers, acquired an impressive
bankroll.
Older now, I'm at a park waiting for a new client.
A kid who lost his brother, resulting in a mindset
erratic and defiant.
He's changed since then fixed on a fresh start.

Hopes for some closure, he's weighted by a heavy heart.

He arrives and plops on the bench next to me.

We introduce ourselves, he with the confidence of an emcee.

"I need to know my brother's all right."

"Sure, not a problem, I'll check, sit tight."

Close my eyes, call the deceased forward from wherever he rests.

The tingling consumes me, I mutter a few questions, basically tests.

Making sure the ghost's identity is legit.

I've dealt with tricksters, pretending, counterfeit.

My client asks, "Why do you close your eyes, what are you doing?"

I open them, say, "I'm trying to reach your brother, sort of, interviewing."

My client squints, obviously confused.

I ask him, "Are you too emotional, do you need to be excused?"

"No," he says with a curled lip. "How can you talk to my brother from here?"

"I'm a medium," I reply, "I tap into the afterlife. I have a supernatural ear."

"My brother's in the hospital, he fell, has a concussion.

Saw him for a moment, but couldn't have a discussion.
I asked you to drop in on him, and you misunderstood, you've misread.
Because I'm the one from the other side, the brother who is dead."

Winter

Some stranger keeps building a snowman outside,
in my backyard, and it's tall and wide,
with a pinecone nose and rock eyes ink dyed.
My parents think it's me but it's not, they say I've
lied.
They're worried the isolation affects me too
much,
according to them, it's why I tell stories and such.
But I don't that's the problem, they're the ones
out of touch.
Forget about them, it's Frosty's maker I want to
clutch.
I wake up in the morning and weirdly it's there.
Three huge snowballs piled high, a nature made
face, vertical stick hair.
I didn't do it, I slept all night, I swear.
And logically it can't just appear from thin air.
I've tried to stay up and catch the trespasser,
who seems to be more of a midnight harasser.
My eyelids got heavy, a dream realm crasher,
I passed out, every time, missed the stealthy yard
dasher.

I've also inspected the rest of the yard,
in the daylight with the sun shining hard.
No footprints, or tracks, the ground was
unmarred.
I'm determined to end this, I'm on guard.
Blizzards keep us trapped here, can't buy Red
Bull.
Tonight, I had some of Mom's coffee, a whole
cupful.
Put on my thick socks, boots, and a warm
sweater, it's wool.
Sit in the window on a stumpy footstool.
At exactly 3a.m. a bunch of snow rolls into a ball,
but no one is there, no person big or small.
I almost holler for my parents down the hall,
to come witness, but instead I stall.
Continue to watch the unbelievable act,
of a snowman building itself, each section
stacked.
And everything placed perfectly, eyes, nose, hair,
arms intact.
When it's done, I can't help but react.
Bundled up and ready to go,
I run outside in the bitter snow.
Stop at the snowman and yell, "Hello?"
Hoping for an answer from someone in the know.

My breath curls around my nose,
snow is deep, we need to bulldoze.
Not surprised, that's the way it goes,
this time of year, everything's froze.
Near my feet a letter carves, one then two,
and on like that until it reads, "How are you?"
My heart pinballs against my ribcage, don't know
what to do.
Indented again, "You should build a snowman
too."
Under the full moon I see in the dark,
entire sentences, every remark.
Then a smiley face forms, the mouth is an arc,
two berries for eyes, the nose a chunk of tree
bark.
"This can't be happening," I volunteer.
"Tell me who you are, what's going on here?"
From out of the snowman a figure, wispy and
sheer,
floats toward me, halts uncomfortably near.
An itch in my ear, it whispers softly,
"Don't be afraid, I'm between worlds, a detainee.
Many years ago, a rare disease took me.
Lost my breath on a Sunday by the oak tree.
In a snap, my normal life was done,

but, I still missed my friends and longed to have
fun.
Wished for company, someone,
unafraid who wouldn't run.
Here you are my fearless friend.
At least I hope you'll have time to spend.
In weather like this, every day is a weekend.
We could make more snowmen in the yard at each
end."

"Look," I blurt in a serious tone.

"I'll play with you, only because we're both alone.

But you've got to know my mind is blown.

Don't be surprised if our plans get postponed."

Out of the blue, a snowball smacks me in the head.

This ghost isn't deterred in the least by being dead.

I round a ball, too, but hesitate by my buried sled.

"You're transparent. That's not fair." I leave plenty unsaid.

Then the snow gathers into a powdery pile.

A tractor wheel sized ball, I grin like a crocodile.

Help the detainee build another snowman, I mold its profile,

snowwomen too, a bold new style.

The sun slowly creeps up in the sky.

I brush off my clothes and say goodbye.
But not forever, I specify.
I'll be back tonight with a bucket of supplies.
Our dozen snow people are well crafted and day-lit.
The yard is a stunning winter exhibit.
My parents are awestruck, ask how I did it.
I reply, "With my friend, a fun-loving spirit."
They shake their heads, take another look at my work.
Mom drops her coffee, Dad doesn't jerk.
Their lips quiver, they're unable to talk.
I gaze outside, I'm stunned too, can't help it, I gawk.
Tears ooze from the eyes of every snowperson—I hear my heart thud.
Not melting ice, or tar, or mud, but streams of glistening blood.

Uninvited

Outside for a hike, doing my thing,
iPhone in hand to snap pics of blooms in spring.
By a scraggy bush, a patch of wildflowers grow,
yellows, and pinks, and one bright as a tomato.
I inhale the fragrance, earthy and sweet,
admire the pods striping healthy mesquite.
I stop, aim my camera, shoot like a pro.
And then to the left, I see before they mow...
a field of bluebonnets jiggling in the breeze,
I step closer, find an interesting angle, prop on
my knees.
Take a few shots, I do this with ease.
Dotting the petals like snowflakes are bees.
My gaze is snagged by a hawk in the sky,
who lands on a branch about ten feet high.
I frame the bird of prey on my phone screen,
pause a minute to stand and wipe it clean.
Refocus and snap auburn feathers against leaves
mossy green.
Nature is my getaway; I find it serene.
Never walked this field before today.
Luckily, it wasn't too far away.

As I scan the environment chills pinch my skin.
Less soothing, more like a morgue—I'm
assuming, I've never been.
A pretty place, peaceful, though I sense I'm not
alone.
I mean, I am, I'm here on my own.
Great! Now there's no signal on my phone.
Irritated, I kick a stone.
My stomach flutters, rapidly, severe.
Going home to shake off this gripping fear.
An hour later I'm seated on my bed,
eating a piece of pumpkin bread,
realizing how my poor judgment lead
me to believe there was something to dread.
My phone works again too, major relief.
Didn't lose my pictures, saves me a ton of grief.
Scrolling through images I don't remember
taking.
Some so grotesque, they've got me shaking.
Within the rainbow of wildflowers, a gauzy face,
painstaking,
its eyes black holes, its mouth slithering worms,
I'm not mistaking.
Panic coils in my throat.
I scroll more, and regrettably note,

A different face, translucent, with needle teeth, demonic,
glowering from under an abnormally large bluebonnet.
Goose pimples prickle every inch of my flesh.
I turn off my phone, try to refresh.
Nothing changes, the horrible faces still exist.
Another next to the hawk in a smoky mist.
Muddled, I wonder how they got there.
Chew my thumbnail, didn't ask for this eerie souvenir.
Stare again at the images raiding my phone,
hideous expressions, I'm in the Twilight Zone.
Following a few moments of serious thought, I decide,
to make the pics public, let me friends preside.
But as I upload to my Insta account,
everything publishes faceless, my stress begins to mount.
I raise my head contemplating what to do next,
and on my dresser mirror, the invisible crafts spooky text.
Our little secret, don't tell a soul.
My pulse races, this is out of control.
I gaze at my phone, and again, I scroll.

The monstrous faces vanished into some unearthly sinkhole.

No evidence, I'm silenced, or risk sounding crazy.

My mouth is dry; eyeballs, probably glazy.

I mutter, "I'm never going back to that creepy meadow."

A disembodied voice rumbles in stereo,

"Stay off our property unless you want torment for years."

The entity further declares, *"Hush, hush, no public shares,*

or we'll haunt you forever with our wicked sneers."

I reply, "No one invited you in my personal spaces,

my phone, my room with your morbid faces.

I agree to respect your boundaries, providing you respect mine too."

Purse my lips and seconds later, just a few,

the mirror text disappears, proving we're through.

We drew a line in the atmosphere.

I won't cross there; they won't cross here.

Switch

One day after school a note blew to my feet.
I bent down, picked it up, read it privately,
discrete.
Written by a kid who said he was my age,
claiming to live in a cabin with a studio and a
batting cage.
The message clearly stated, if I walked forward
into the forest, the deepest part,
I'd run into a house, walls covered in impressive
abstract art.
Boggled how he learned I liked to draw and paint,
and that I played baseball, and lacked restraint.
Reasons why I'd be willing to explore this hidden
place,
go on an adventure, I had my switchblade just in
case.
Left my friends and marched into the woods,
every step I took,
I'd look for a detailed map, guidebook, or spying
crook.
Buttery dots of sunlight melted on the leaves,

a glittery trail I followed, hoping it wouldn't bring
me to thieves.
Or worse. Some too terrifying to think.
I continued hiking uphill, knife in hand, refusing
to blink.
Humid as a sauna, sweat burned my eyes,
tension in my muscles, unexpected exercise.
I kept going, dirt and grass under my shoes.
Figured why not? I had nothing to lose.
Was whistling a song when a guy came out of
nowhere,
with bell-bottom blue jeans and shoulder-length
hair.
"Dude, you made it," he said, "I hit a homerun.
Sent a couple letters, but couldn't get anyone to
come."
I replied, "Here I am, let's see this so-called cabin.
I'm overheated, dying of thirst, as you can
imagine."
"Yeah, yeah," he said, "but let me ask you a
question first,
you know, before we take care of your
bothersome thirst."
I shrugged too tired to argue and honestly, I was
interested.
What did this person want, what had I elicited?

He said, "By the way, toss the knife, it won't help you survive.

You're in a land of wonder, I can't even begin to describe."

A lightning bolt of realty shot through my brain.

I'd stumbled into trouble, but he wasn't hostile or outwardly insane.

"Tell you what," I said, "Nix the cabin, the batting cage or whatever you had to share,

I'm leaving and if you try and stop me, if you dare,

maybe a blade you don't fear, but my fists will put you six feet under, you and your stupid stare."

I backtracked the regrettable steps I had taken.

He joined me, a mime, copied my movements, completely unshaken.

Twigs snapped beneath my soles, rabbits scurried, heat singed my skin.

The kid wouldn't leave my side, he behaved mechanical, a coldblooded twin.

As we reached the forest's edge my school located just beyond

parked cars and the fountain with more algae than a pond.

I turned to him and asked, "Earlier you had a question, is it still on your mind?"

Couldn't explain, but his hair and clothes
changed. Had I been blind?
He looked familiar, a lot like me.
He said, "Do you believe in curses, evil promises
or an unholy plea?"
"What are talking about?" I asked pushing my
blade in his face.
"Now you sound kooky, a freakin' mental case."
He said, "You're not going to like what I have to
say at all,
centuries ago, sometime in the fall.
An old blacksmith's son met with a drunken mob,
who guzzled moonshine, and considered the son
a snob.
They tied him up and did terrible things.
Tortured him to death, brought the blacksmith
his son's rings.
The old man retaliated, shot them all dead.
Searched for his son's body with no luck, not a
thread.
'A boy for a boy,' he screamed in the night.
'From this point on, the woods will keep one, make
this wrong right.
The first will be me, I'll stay here, die with my child.
Until a trade can be made with one easily
beguiled.'"

I scratched my head somewhat amused.

None of it mattered, not staying, I refused.

I asked, "How long have you been here, a day, two, or three?"

My twin said, "I wish. Since 1970.

It took this long to find paper and pen,

and someone to lure, I tried, again and again."

I chuckled and said, "It's been a riot, but I've got to go."

Turned to step on the concrete, my foot flopped, gooey as cookie dough.

My muscles mushy, body weighed some zillion pounds.

I couldn't leave the forest; I was trapped on the grounds.

My crazy twin smiled and snidely winked, followed by a sound, something clinked.

It was my switchblade now in his hand.

He was me, I didn't understand.

He shrugged and said, "It's been a riot, but I've got to go."

Then strode out of the woods with ease, a calm flow.

Hopped on my bike, gone in a minute.

I bawled, exceeding my coping limit.

Apparently, I'd be here a while,

until a trade could be made, my nightmarish exile.

Besties

In the hospital two months today,
another kid, my best friend, is in Bed B, I'm in
Bed A.
Medications zap our energy,
both of us tired, Bed B and me.
"A," I hear in the room from Bed B,
"It's too quiet right now, turn on the TV."
"Sure," I answer, and click on an interesting
program,
the Travel Channel airing a parade in Amsterdam.
We like to see what's going on outside of this
place,
and in the rest of the world, including space.
Any show that helps us forget,
we're hooked to IVs, dodging a medical death
threat.
Books are cool, but sometimes can't focus.
Found an app online, learning self-hypnosis.
Claims to relieve pain, it's not working yet.
Bed B tried it too, said it's an app we should
forget.
Me and my friend who rests in Bed B,

bonded overnight, having similar challenges, practically.

"Hey, B, when we're discharged, we should go on a trip,

celebrate with our families on a luxury cruise ship."

"That would be awesome, can't wait for the day, when we can plan a getaway.

Keep checking your cheeks for coloring light pink.

And brighter eyes, signals you're healing, I think."

"Whoa, B, I appreciate you trying to keep me out of the grave.

You're not a doctor, but opinions are all the rave.

We're both struck with a similar curse,

but you're pretty bossy, so yours might be worse."

We giggle from the pits of our stomachs,

obviously overtired because we each see strange flecks.

"B, are you sleepy? My eyes need to close."

But B's already in the dreamland throes.

Seems like we just fell asleep, and we're already awake,

me and B jump out of bed without a single ache.

"B, I don't hurt anymore, how about you?"

"Yeah, I'm not in pain, I feel better too."

I swing my hips, perform a nerdy dance.
"Look, B, I've got termites in my underpants."
"And a stain free hospital gown.
My parents will be ecstatic; I'm so over seeing
them down."
"B, your face has color, some kind of magic,
we're strong, active, no longer sick."
I turn toward the bathroom to look in the mirror,
see if my face is less pale but as I get nearer,
I notice a crowd in our room and they're crying,
then I recognize it's our families muttering about
dying.
"We're here," I wave. "We're a hundred percent
fine."
I stand by the window, in the sun, its warm
golden shine.
B points to our beds, her eyes bugging weird.
My gaze follows her finger, everything we once
feared.
There we were under the sheets ashen and
motionless,
our parents torn up, suddenly childless.
But we can't complain, we've got plenty of gusto.
"Hey, B," I say. "Want to watch a different show?"
B nods yes and grabs the remote,
changes the channel to a series on a houseboat.

The adults in the room gasp and scream,
complete shambles, into the hallway they stream.
They're inconsolable, we feel bad for their
heartbreak,
but we agree we're better off, neither of us ache.
We have each other, we're equally clever.
Bed A and Bed B, best friends forever.

Spooked

Long time ago something bad happened to me.
Not important anymore, it's a distant memory.
You see, it's okay being stuck in a Fun House of
mirrors, tunnels, and ramps,
with crazy glow in the dark lighting cast by
hidden lamps.
Like me, that's what I do, I hide in the dark,
waiting for bold kids visiting the amusement
park.
They think they're tough and hard to scare,
but the minute I yank or breathe in their hair,
they scream like big babies and scatter back out
there,
where they belong with their mommies
whispering prayer.
Tonight's big, a unique event.
Can't wait for unsuspecting newcomers to
torment.
I overheard something about a special needs
school.
Easy targets, terrifying them will be cool.
Sounds move closer, laughter and dumb noises,

the loud girls and boys is
heading this way for a night they'll never forget.
Glide to my positon, planning my best scares yet.
I dissolve in the wall and wait for my first victim.
Oh, yeah, I see one, no second thoughts, his
future is grim.
He's in a wheelchair with a bulky bag on his lap.
I'll make him cry and drop it, he's rolling into a
trap.
As I wait anxiously in the void,
he wheels closer, looking annoyed.
Almost as if he could see me, but I know that's
impossible.
I reach through the purple plywood, I'm
unstoppable.
Touch his knee, expecting him to pee,
instead, he stares directly at me.
Smirks, and talks as if I'm not scary.
He says, "I don't know what you're trying to do,
but touch me again and you'll be begging for
tissue,
to wipe your crybaby eyes.
I've got exceptional tools to utilize."
Then he dunked his hand in his bag,
pulled out a square gadget and began to brag,

"I'm not afraid of you, but you need to be careful of me,

I'm a ghost hunter, and by that, I mean, I could set you free,

from this place, indefinitely, make me mad and you'll see.

So, if this is where you want to be,

don't mess with this paranormal devotee."

Can't believe this punk in a chair,

acting like he doesn't care.

I'll show him, got a trick up my sleeve.

My face pushes through the wall, I snarl, sure to make him leave.

Instead, he growls loud,

like a bursting thunderous cloud.

Freaking me out.

Now, I'm filled with doubt.

But I try again with a raging shout.

I yell, "Get out! Get out! Get out!"

He points his gadget in my direction.

It beeps, and clicks, and cramps my midsection.

Clinching my stomach, I ask, "What are you doing?"

He says, "My invention, it's your energy I'm ungluing."

Time to retreat, I sink back in the wall.

My essence is shaking, met my near downfall.
I'm tangled up, all confused,
described in a word I've never used.
Terrified—first time it's happened to me here.
His laughter echoes as he creaks away in his
wheelchair.

Routine

Don't think I've ever cried this hard,
my dog just died, we buried him in the yard.
He had a long happy life, fifteen years.
Knew this was coming, but no one truly prepares.
My eyes sting, stomach knots, chest sinks
repeatedly,
different than earlier when I reacted heatedly.
We found him wandering the streets when he was
young.
Just a pup, scooped him up, he slobbered my
cheek with his tongue.
We grew together, swam and hiked,
he ran next to me when I biked.
Never thought it'd be this grueling to say
goodbye,
but damn, it is, here to testify.
One silver lining is he's not suffering anymore.
As much as it annoyed me, I'll miss his earth-
shaking snore.
And throwing a Frisbee,
chilling in front of the TV,
watching him roll in the grass carefree.
Out of breath, I'm drowning undersea.

Need shut-eye, sleep through the pain.
Hit the bed, and then something I can't explain...
Heaviness and warmth across my feet,
same section my dog slept, recognize the body
heat.
The weight quickly shifts to the right side.
My heart races, an unexpected emotional ride.
Open my eyes, check for the cause.
Nothing there, but the shape of his paws.
Four indents on the quilt as if he stood watching
me,
the way he did weekend mornings, the only time
we'd disagree.
He'd want me up, I'd want to sleep,
moments later I'd throw a ball, high, he liked to
leap.
Hop out of bed, this can't be real.
Pressure against my leg, exactly the way he'd heel.
The comfort he gave I'm feeling again.
It's strange, beyond my ken.
Smell him too, his stinky sweat.
Crouch, catch a breeze, wagging his tail I bet.
Hear myself talk, I sound like a freak.
Then a wet sensation swipes my cheek.
Place my hand on my face, saliva, it's him.
My dog is back, but unlike a phantom limb,

it's more than a feeling, he's positively here.
Bringing me his empty food bowl; it's floating in
midair.

Writer

Once upon a time in the dark mangled woods,
a creature formed from discarded hardgoods.
Scratch that, not the story I want to tell.
Doesn't sound original, it'd be tough to sell.
I have my notepad and fancy pen.
Prefer writing by hand but then again,
the laptop is quicker, easier to get things done,
not my goal though, at least not for page one.
Disjointed thoughts need to streamline on paper.
Starts out rough, and then I, the story shaper,
can edit, revise, make it a mystery,
or horror or romance or insert whimsical history.
A bonus worth mentioning regarding a notepad
over a computer,
is some places I go lack internet access and a
troubleshooter.
This moment, for example, I'm in my aunt's
spooky attic.
Inspirational location, it's genuinely enigmatic.
Not the space, but the objects my aunt said were
here before her,
antique Barbie dolls, bald, with wigs soft as fur.
Desks, books, and lots of clothes,

a sweatshirt with a tiger on the front, its face,
eyes, mouth, and nose.
There's also a mattress in front of the window.
I'm sitting on it, comfortable, hoping to escape
author limbo.
Cobwebs lacing the beams above,
provide ideas, a mental shove.
Press my pen to the paper and thoughtfully
write...
A slender shadow drifts, only seen at night.
Munching on spiders and mice and mold—
When suddenly my pen moves against my hold.
My heart races, I release the pen.
It glides on its own writing words and then,
the notepad floats in front of my face and I read,
Spiders and mice? Never, guaranteed.
My mouth falls open, fingers tremble,
takes a minute, but my scattered thoughts
reassemble.
From my gaping lips, I manage to say,
"I should probably run, but I can't look away."
More writing, hard to believe what I see.
Impossible to rationalize this unbelievable
anomaly.
My brain whirs in static shock.
Overwhelming experience, I stiffen like a rock.

Finally, the pad is upright, and again I read,
Once upon a time, there was a girl that could bleed,
made of bones, skin, hope, and joyous laughter,
her life before the hereafter.
She grew ill but remained optimistic,
despite the doctors who were sadly fatalistic.
Her parents cried endless rivers of tears,
the grief went on for several years.
Until dismally, on an unforgettable day,
the girl peacefully slipped away.
Soon, a strangeness occurred, her laughter returned.
She scanned her environment, she wasn't concerned.
The attic she played in before she died,
in the house settled by the lakeside,
is where she'll stay for the rest of her afterlife.
She doesn't mind, no turmoil or strife.
The attic is compelling with plenty to do.
Barbie's are her favorite, but she treasures the books too.
Not a scary spirit, though if she were forced to leave,
she'd fit and rage, every object she would heave,
and throw and break, and make targets of guests,

who choose to be unkind and transform into pests.
Not a threat, more a warning, or something to
ponder.
Don't try to modify, let the spectral wander.
So, this is the story to compose, and depending
how you act,
will determine how frightening, how strong the
impact.
There's even a title, and it's not too dramatic.
For obvious reasons, we'll call it Ghost in the Attic.
The notepad drops to the mattress I'm on.
I snatch it, rush out, I want to be gone.
Fumble downstairs to the table to assess,
what just happened, I'm kind of a mess.
As my jumbled nerves solidly relax,
I go to the pantry, grab a handful of snacks.
A fire is burning deep within.
I'm motivated, ready to begin,
the paranormal tale, my passionate plight,
one of a ghost in the attic who likes to write.

Instrumental

Awoke to the sound of a heavy bass beat,
coming from somewhere at the end of my street.
We live on a culdesac, so I can't imagine,
where the music is coming from, but I plan to
examine.
Walking that way, strange, no one is complaining,
'bout the blaring tunes, I find entertaining.
Doesn't matter to me, I like to jam.
Excited 'bout neighbors who are the same as I am.
Pass a few houses, missing kid signs outside,
the beat rattles my bones; the music's amplified.
Made it here, where my street ends,
met by a cool treehouse, that sort of blends
with the woods and leaves, but where'd it come
from?
It wasn't here yesterday spitting out this hypnotic
thrum.
I gaze skyward. "Anybody there?"
No one answers, they probably can't hear.
On the rope ladder, rusty bells are attached,
I give it a shake, before an idea is hatched.
Climb the twine rungs and knuckle the door,
then peek through a window, there are four.

Fatigue green curtains keep the inside concealed.
I turn the knob, wish I had a shield,
in case someone overreacts, uses a weapon.
Taking a chance, through the doorway, I step in.
The blasting music stops, but I don't see anyone,
or a sound system, definitely, none.
Walls and floors are smooth and clean,
two beanbag cushions, and those curtains, army
green.
Other than that, the place is an empty square.
I'm worried, 'cause I know the rhythms came
from here.
A pine aroma invades my nose,
considering where I'm at, makes sense, I suppose.
I stroll the interior trying to understand,
how a short while ago banging beats took
command.
Nothing here, dumbfounded, I can't explain.
Gonna sit down, relieve mental strain.
In a shadowy corner, I sink in a beanbag,
recount events for a possible red flag.
The music that played pulled me out of my house,
brought me here, like cheese does a mouse.
My stomach churns, I stand to desert this place.
Rip open the door, blood drains from my face.
I gasp at the images staring back at me,

other teens in doorways of houses in trees.
We're all suspended in some vacuum, indistinct.
whaling, confused, somehow we're linked.
My heart pounds painfully, a drum in my chest.
Shaky and scared, I'm totally stressed.
My heart bangs even louder, I doubt it's mine,
until the other teens hearts throb in sync, a
chilling band line.
Our heartbeats increase in volume and pace,
with unintentional cadence and grace.
My cheeks are on fire from my body's rising heat.
Realizing what caused the heavy bass beat.

Signs

Said goodbye to Grandpa today,
in a blue silk-lined coffin he lay.
A gentle color, like the sky.
Soothed me after an exhausting cry.
The blue matched his eyes, which always looked
at me with love.
I know deep down he's watching me from above.
Left the adults to converse by themselves,
to check out the books stuffed on crooked
shelves.
They were in a small room with carpet orange-
ish-red,
which instantly reminded me of Grandpa's head.
His hair like ginger, curly and funny.
He always told jokes, called Grandma his Sweet
Honey.
Back to the books, one had pages of cars.
Grandpa raced off-road, won golden stars.
I sat on a bench and gazed out the window,
then a crow jumped down from the willow.
Cawed a few times, stretched his wings in the
sun.

Crows were Grandpa's favorite, he fed them chunks of watermelon.

He used to recite a poem when the sprinklers hit his garden.

Unexpected rain claps the ground as if the drops were hardened.

Grandpa drank black coffee, and suddenly its aroma fills the air.

His body may be gone, but now he exists everywhere.

Unbound

Moved to this city a few weeks ago,
something we do a lot, wish we'd win lotto.
Dad got let go from another job,
Mom's on disability, on the couch like a blob.
Can't help it, I get mad about the cards I was
dealt.
Wish they placed me for adoption, not gonna lie,
that's how I've felt
for too long, tired of this life,
where heartache and struggle are rife.
Out exploring my rough neighborhood,
deteriorating homes, shady people, the challenges
of my childhood.
I have a phone, texted some of my friends last
night,
since I'm in a different district, they said we're no
longer tight.
Now I'm out walking, aware of my warped world
view.
Trust me, it's messed up, I feel doomed, don't
have a clue.
Across the street in front of a vacant warehouse,

two little kids jump rope, one in a dress, the other in jeans and a pink blouse.

I glance up and down the street for their parents or an older sibling.

Five or six is too young to be alone by that building.

Jog over there, yell, "Hey, where's your folks?"

The kids drop their rope, scurry inside, playing jokes.

Now I'm worried they'll get hurt or killed, goosebumps pinch my skin, I feel unskilled.

Hurry in after them to make sure they're alright.

The place is filthy, charred, not much light.

A fire had torched everything inside.

Have to find the kids who apparently like to hide.

"Look, I'm not a bad guy just concerned about you.

Shouldn't be in here, it's nasty, dangerous, and stinks like mildew."

From behind a blackened cabinet emerge two small faces.

The kids who jumped rope, and then, near slanted bookcases,

six more kids, three on each side,

took measured steps into the open, I'm stumped, I confide.

"Man, what's going on here, you kids better tell me
why you're in this death trap? Where's your family?"
As my vision focuses I see chalkboards and desks.
Must have been a school or daycare is my best guess.
More young kids come out from every corner of the room,
a total of fifteen, eyes glassy with gloom.
"This is crazy, you know." I rub my head,
frustrated no one looked for them, not a tear shed.
I ask, "What's your story, what gives?"
A boy says, *"This is where we live."*
Followed by a girl who utters, *"It's our home... inside, back and front yard, that's as far as we're allowed to roam."*
I say, "Too weird. I'm calling a cop."
Then the kids vanish, for real, no Photoshop.
I want to take off, but I'm mystified, I observe,
the kids reappearing, mind tricks I don't deserve.
Tried to snap a picture, but they disappear again.
Wasn't worth the effort, bigger concerns in this dangerous playpen.
"Okay, this is nuts, someone better explain.

This ain't a nice thing to do to anyone's brain."
Within the sooty enclosure, the kids shoot me a
pointed stare,
and it finally dawns on me they truly are stuck
here.
"If I didn't witness you with my own two eyes,
I wouldn't believe it, even if someone told me,
couldn't visualize.
Ghosts, right?"
A boy nods, his face etched with fright.
"You're all as real as you could be in this sad
space,
unfortunately, it's not a situation I can erase.
I'm sorry for you kids, but I can't wrap my mind
around this place."
A young girl in blue says, *"I don't remember what
happened to me...
crying for Mommy is all I can remember or see...
we were taking naps—"*
With a swell in my throat, I interrupt, "So
peacefully."
I shake my head,
queasy, communicating with the dead.
Before I turn toward the door,
a young spirit hands me a book titled: A Day at
The Toy Store.

She asks, *"Would you read us a story, it would help us rest?*
We're always wandering, you're our only guest,
to see us, you must be special or blessed."
"Or hexed," I mumble, still rightly skewed.
I add, "I'm alive, in that regard, I have gratitude."
From across the room, a chair slides close to my knees.
A weepy girl asks, *"Please?"*
And then, *"Do we have to beg?"* A boy asks with a frown.
Urges me to stay in this contained ghost town.
Slowly I sit, as far as issues go, this is the crux.
Ghostly kids huddle at my feet, I'm nervous, my reading sucks.
I take the book from a transparent schoolboy,
reminding myself they're desperate for joy.
Start making out words in this tale of a toy store,
sounding out syllables, the kids are kind to ignore my inability to read well,
but the setting squeezes me out of my shell.
One by one, the kids close their eyes, gently fall asleep.
I no longer feel like an angry black sheep,
but a person who might have something to offer this imperfect world.

Ideas about my future unfurled and swirled.

Fast forward... a year later,

I quit calling myself a hater.

I visited the ghost kids every day.

With each story one of the spirits made their way
to the other side, where peace could be found.

In the old, burned school, they were no longer
bound.

Me neither, I'm free from my doom.

Reading gave me confidence, hope, not destined
for an early tomb.

Going to be a writer or teacher to give kids like
me a chance.

We're not bad, but like my ghost friends, we're
victims of circumstance.

Contrary to them, I could make the changes
necessary to succeed.

Create the life I dreamed about, feeling positive
now that I could read.

About the Author

L. Buckley writes horror and dark fiction books and screenplays. She lives in Texas with her husband and a menagerie of rescue animals.